To order additional copies of this book, contact:
Xlibris
844-714-8691
www.Xlibris.com
Orders@Xlibris.com

ISBN: Softcover   978-1-4535-5913-0
        EBook   978-1-6698-6454-7

Print information available on the last page

Rev. date: 01/25/2023

Kayla could not sleep,

Her eyes would not shut.

Her toes were so restless,

As was Billy, her mutt.

"The covers are warm mommy,
I haven't made a peep.
But no matter what I try,
I can't fall asleep!"

"There's one thing I know," said mommy,
Which works every time.
We'll call Dr. Sleepy,

He's an old friend of mine."

And then he appeared,
Riding a big fluffy,
white cloud.

"I'm the Doctor of Dreams,"
He stated out loud.

"The Sultan of Sleep.
The Supervisor of Snooze.
The Director of Dreams,
Here to take away those 'can't get to sleep'
Blues."

"Why, it's easy to fall asleep, Kayla,
Once you know how.
Just listen to Doc Sleepy,
Pay attention to me now!"

"Get ready to dream Kayla,
Cause dreaming is the key.
It will make you sleepy,
From your head to your knees."

"You can dream about happy thoughts.
Funny thoughts, and silly thoughts too.
You can dream in different colors - red,
Green, or blue!"

"You can dream about puppies,
parakeets, or cats.

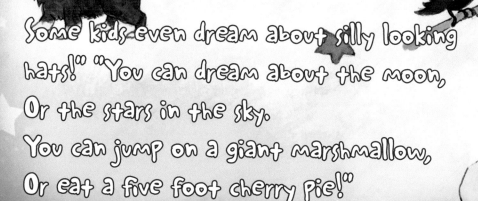

Some kids even dream about silly looking
hats!" "You can dream about the moon,
Or the stars in the sky.
You can jump on a giant marshmallow,
Or eat a five foot cherry pie!"

5

Now Kayla was not quite sure
Of this physician extraordinaire,
With his round, blue face,
And purplish green hair.

"How can **he** make me sleep?

How can **he** make me drowsy?

What if **his** dreams are really quite lousy?"

With that, Dr. Sleepy zoomed down to the Bed.
"Kayla, don't let those thoughts dance in your Head.
I have the cure, the Prescription you need.

You'll be asleep fast.   Just follow my lead."

"Now close those eyes, Kayla.

Take a deep breath .

Stretch the big, big, stretch .

Flumple your tummy.

And tickle your neck!"

"We're off to Dreamland, Kayla.
And keep those eyes closed'
You'll do that to see there,
As everyone knows."
"For in Dreamland it's different
Than your room at night.
Your eyes have to be **closed**
To see all the sights"
And with that Kayla started to dream.
Her head was now tired; she had run out
Of steam.
The stretching had worked,
Her tummy was flumpled.
Her body was quiet, under those covers
So rumpled.

Suddenly, just in front of Kayla,

At the top of the hill,

SLEEPYVILLE

Stood an entrance to a wonderful place

A place Dr. Sleepy called Sleepyville!

"Come right on in," said Doc.

"This is the first stop in Dreamland.

Here you can fly,

or jump,

or run.

You can do whatever you want to.
Just use your imagination!"

SLEEPYVILLE

Kayla passed under the sign of this fantasy place,
Without so much as making a face.

Then her cheeks began to rise,
Her smile began to widen.
She couldn't believe what the
Doc had been Hiding!

The mountains were blue.

Nice to meet you!

The sky was **too!**

There were elephants

and monkeys and a

Silly looking creature

who said, "Nice to meet You"

There was a stream going gurggly - gook.

There was a tree made out of teddy bears,

gurggly

And a pony, reading a book.

There were toys of every shape and kind.

"Come play with us," they said.

"We don't mind!"

"Where did all of this come from Dr. Sleepy?"
Kayla said with a fright.
"Why, it came from you," said Doc.
"It's what you're dreaming tonight"
"The mountains, the sky, the stream, the
Animals .
They came from your head.
And the best part of it is,
You're still in your bed!"

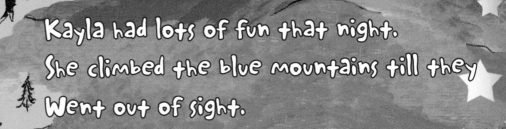

Kayla had lots of fun that night.
She climbed the blue mountains till they
Went out of sight.

She swam in the stream that went
gurggly Gook.

She listened to the pony, as he read his

Favorite book.

She flew on a cloud – clear to the next page

Kayla was having fun,

in lots of different

ways.

She marched with the toys,

And rolled on her back.

Then chased a pink monkey

Down a long, yellow track.

19

She danced with the monkeys, and quickly
found out,

If you step on their tails, they let out a

Big shout!

After awhile, Kayla heard Doc say,
"We're at the end of Dreamland, dear,
It's time for you and your pup
To start to wake up."
"But I'm not ready to go Doc,
I'm having so much fun!
Can't I stay a lrttle longer?"
"That's the great thing about Sleepyville."
Said Doc,
"you can come back tomorrow!"
Kayla jumped on Doc's cloud, and off they
Flew,
Leaving the mountains and the sky so blue.

They zoomed past the monkeys and the teddy Bear tree. Kayla waved at the toys --

"thanks for playing With me!"

22

Their journey was near the end.
Where they began, was just around the bend.
Then Kayla's eyes began to flutter.
Her mouth began to yawn
This night was over,
It was almost dawn.

Her room was quiet.

Dr. Sleepy was nowhere to be found.
But Kayla knew he would still be around.

She remembered what Dr. Sleepy had
Taught her,

She remembered the way to Sleepyville.

THE END

Printed in the United States
by Baker & Taylor Publisher Services